W is for Won...

My First Australian Word Book

Bronwyn Bancroft

LITTLE 🐇 HARE

www.littleharebooks.com

ant hill

ants

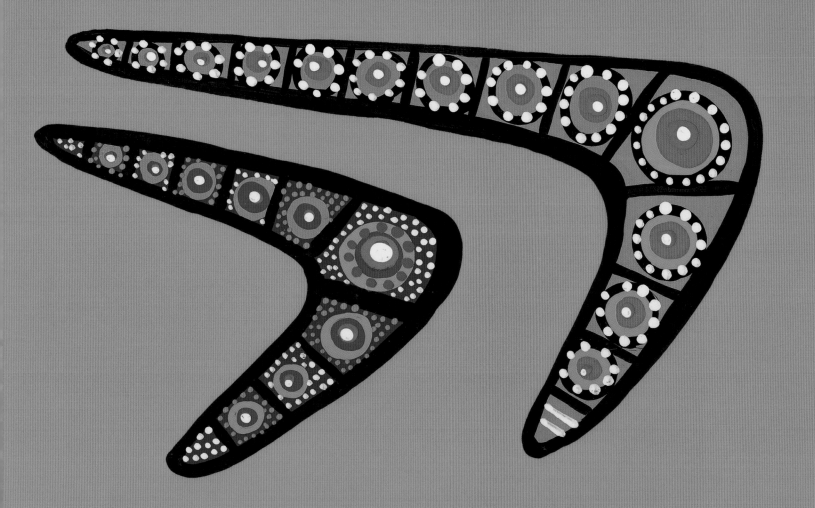

boomerangs

cockatoos

dingo

emu

emu chick

emu eggs

flies

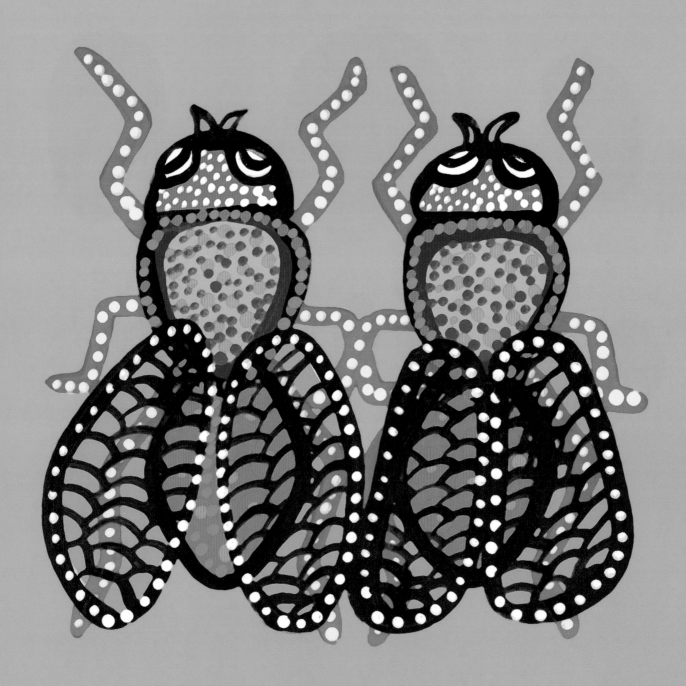

goanna

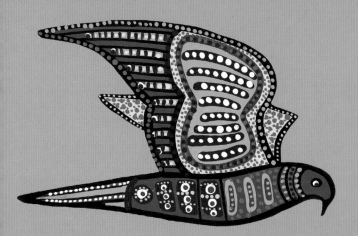

hawk

island

joey

koala

lyrebird

magpie

numbat

owl

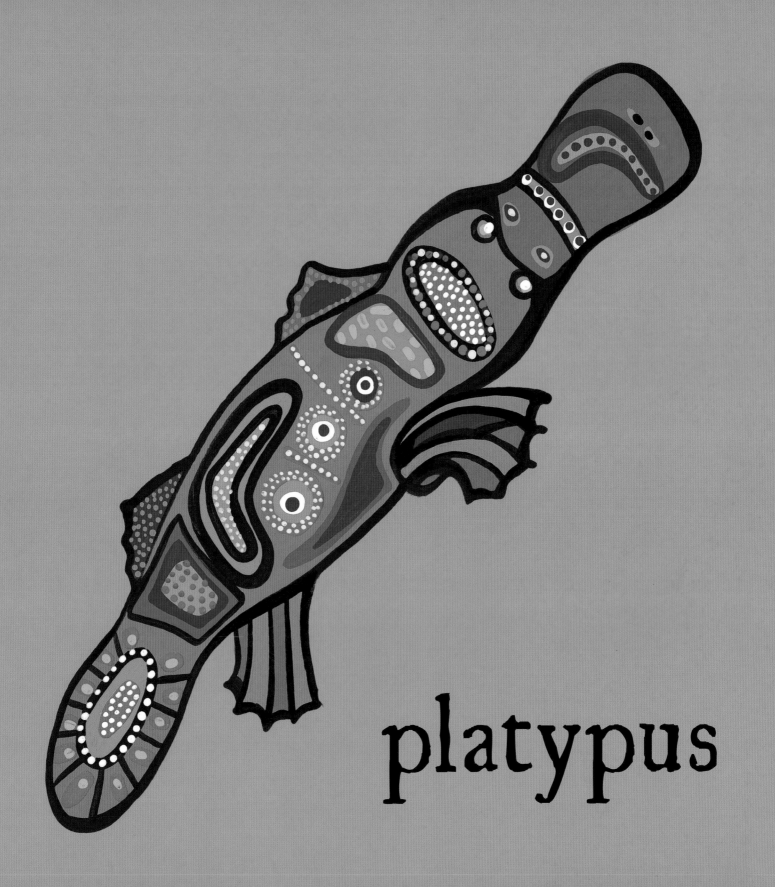

platypus

quokka

river

sun

tree

unicorn fish

vine

wombat

yabby

zebra fish

Bronwyn Bancroft has illustrated several award-winning books for children. Some of her successful books with Little Hare are the highly acclaimed *Possum and Wattle: My Big Book of Australian Words* (shortlisted Queensland Premier's Literary Award 2009; shortlisted Australian Bookseller Association Best Children's Book 2009; listed Children's Book Council of Australia Notable Book 2009), *Malu Kangaroo* (by Judith Morecroft), *An Australian 1, 2, 3 of Animals* and *An Australian abc of Animals*. Bronwyn received the May Gibbs Fellowship from the Dromkeen Centre for Children's Literature in 2000, and was the recipient of the 2009 Dromkeen Medal.

I would like to dedicate this book to two of my close friends: Euphemia Bostock, for her unique and powerful use of words, and Sally Morgan, who taught me the meaning of words—BB

Little Hare Books
an imprint of
Hardie Grant Egmont
85 High Street
Prahran, Victoria 3181, Australia

www.littleharebooks.com

First published 2008
This edition published 2010

National Library of Australia
Cataloguing-in-Publication entry

Bancroft, Bronwyn.
W is for wombat: my first Australian word book / Bronwyn Bancroft.
9781921541858 (pbk.)
For pre-school age.
Alphabet books – Australia – Juvenile literature.
English language – Alphabet – Juvenile literature.
Animals – Australia – Juvenile literature.
Plants – Australia – Juvenile literature.
421.1

Designed by Bernadette Gethings
Produced by Pica Digital, Singapore
Printed through Phoenix Offset
Printed in Shen Zhen, Guangdong Province, China, April 2010

5 4 3 2 1